The Camping Adventure

Frank & Carol Endersby

BUS STOP

© THE MEDICI SOCIETY LTD · LONDON · 1994. Printed in England.
First published in 1991.

ISBN 0 85503 166 2

'Thistleberry Farm!', called the bus driver as the noisy vehicle rounded the bend. Thimble and Bobbin scuttled to their feet as the bus jolted to a halt. Anxiously they peered through the open door and sure enough there was dear Uncle Romsey just as he had promised their mother, standing with little Lily, their cousin. They turned and thanked the bus driver as Uncle Romsey helped them with their luggage. 'Good day to you,' he shouted as the bus trundled off into the distance.

'Welcome to Thistleberry Farm,' said Lily as she hugged Thimble. 'Come along,' urged Uncle Romsey, 'let's find a good spot to pitch this tent.' 'Look – there's the duck pond over there', shouted Thimble. 'Are those the hen houses?' asked Bobbin. 'Yes,' said Uncle Romsey, 'but I don't know what's wrong with the hens at the moment – they're just not laying. I've only had a few eggs all week – very odd is that! Well, what about this spot for your tent?' 'This will be great,' chorused Thimble and Bobbin together.

Uncle Romsey had to return to work, so he left Lily, Thimble and Bobbin in the meadow to pitch the tent and unpack. They were quite used to camping, as they had been many times before, and set to work. Presently Bobbin mused, 'Well, that's the last tent peg in', as he sat back – mallet in hand. Lily helped Thimble arrange the sleeping bags. 'How cosy it looks,' thought Thimble. 'Come on girls – stop day-dreaming,' shouted Bobbin, 'Look, there's Uncle Romsey at the hen house.' They all ran over to him. 'Please may we help?' asked Bobbin. 'Perhaps you can feed these awkward hens,' replied Uncle Romsey 'and I'll be back in a while to see how you're getting along.'

Although the hens had been fed there was still no sign of any eggs. 'Perhaps the hens are unhappy,' said Thimble. 'I know,' replied Bobbin, 'let's go and ask Uncle Romsey if *we* can clean and whitewash the hen house and tidy the chicken run – surely that will please the hens.' Uncle Romsey thought it a splendid idea so they all spent a very enjoyable afternoon transforming the hen house. The hens seemed most impressed with their clean bright home – but still no eggs! Just as the youngsters crossed the farmyard, Bobbin spotted some broken eggshells and an old ladder by the wall. 'Well – the hens have been laying after all,' stammered Thimble, 'so where are all the eggs?'

They busied themselves collecting provisions and dry wood for the camp-fire just as Uncle Romsey returned to light and tend it. They eagerly told him their news of the discovered eggshells and ladder. 'I think we'll put a plan into action later tonight,' he retorted, 'but first let's eat – I'm famished!' A wonderful smell wafted from the iron pot above the fire. They hungrily devoured the stew bubbling within and washed it down with home-made ginger beer. Then what a rousing sing-song they had – verse after verse of everyone's favourite songs!

It was much later on that Uncle Romsey announced, 'What a splendid evening – I haven't enjoyed myself so much for ages. Now what do you think of my plan to keep watch over the hen house tonight?' The young rabbits were quite excited about the proposed vigil. Uncle Romsey provided his largest torch and a sleeping bag for Lily. He put out the glowing embers of the camp-fire. 'Be careful,' he warned, 'and if you see anything suspicious just shout – I won't be far away.'

'Gosh, it's very dark,' whispered
Thimble, 'What's that noise?'
They all listened, 'It's only the
wind,' said Lily, 'Don't worry.' As
time passed they all felt very tired.
'Let's lie down in our sleeping
bags,' urged Thimble, 'We can tie
back the tent flaps and still listen.'
Bobbin thought about it, 'All
right then – just for a while', he said hesitantly. No sooner
had they snuggled down into their sleeping bags than they
heard a noise outside – but it was only the hoot of an owl and
eventually one by one they drifted off to sleep.

'Quickly,' commanded Bobbin, 'get the torch – what's that scuffling noise outside?' They half stumbled out of the tent and flashed on the torch beam across the meadow. Right in its path were two nasty looking characters up to no good. 'Look,' shouted Bobbin, 'they're raiding the hen house!' The chickens were in uproar. The youngsters rushed from their tent shouting loudly 'Hey, stop thieves!' The two figures were so startled that they ran off at once. Bobbin and the girls gave chase around the meadow running in circles until the clatter of pots and pans could be heard as the two thieves tripped over the tent pegs and crashed to the ground.

A large figure stepped out of the shadows. 'Well, what do we have here?' boomed Uncle Romsey. 'If it isn't Wriggler and Rascal Rat', he said, grabbing each by the scruff of the neck as they wriggled and squirmed. 'Here's the reason why you've had no eggs', panted Bobbin as he approached. 'Yes,' gasped Thimble, 'and we've caught them red-handed!' 'Look, their baskets, full with our eggs, are still by the hen house', shouted Lily as she caught them all up. 'Mmmm,' grunted Uncle Romsey, 'I'm handing them over to PC Brock – let's see what he has to say about this. Well done, Bobbin, Thimble and Lily, I'll catch up with you three at breakfast.' And off he marched the rats towards the farmhouse.

Later that morning Thimble, Lily and Bobbin sat down to a huge breakfast in the farmhouse kitchen cooked by Aunt Flossie. Just then there was a knock on the door and in walked PC Brock. 'Good morning,' he said, 'I've just called round to let you know that Wriggler and Rascal Rat have both confessed. Quite a clever plan it seems — stealing your eggs at night into their  baskets, passing them over the wall to each other to load into their barrow. Then it was off to market early each morning to sell them and make their money. They will, of course, be punished and are very sorry for what they have done.' 'Well, thank you for your help everyone,' said Uncle Romsey, 'Or I could say — you've certainly cracked that one!'